For Jude and Barry, with love - T. C. x

For my little nephew, Isaac - T. W. x

tiger tales

5 River Road, Suite 128, Wilton, CT 06897
Published in the United States 2016
Originally published in Great Britain 2016
by Little Tiger Press
Text copyright © 2016 Tracey Corderoy
Illustrations copyright © 2016 Tim Warnes
Visit Tim Warnes at www.ChapmanandWarnes.com
ISBN-13: 978-1-68010-033-4
ISBN-10: 1-68010-033-5
Printed in China
LTP/1400/1437/0216

For more insight and activities, visit us at www.tigertalesbooks.com

NOW!

by Tracey Corderoy

Illustrated by Tim Warnes

tiger tales

Otto found waiting
a little bit hard.

He wanted to have all the fun **NOW!**

Each day was full of exciting things.
And when did Otto want them . . . ?

But even Otto had to agree that **"NOW!"** wasn't always best . . . .

Then one day Mom had exciting news.
They were going on vacation!

To help Otto wait, they made a count-down chart. Dad used his special pens.

But who is going to cross off the days?

ME!

They played airplanes,
too . . .

and made a
jumbo jet model.

As Otto crossed off the days, he became
more and more excited . . . .

Finally, it was time to go!

Except
there was one **BIG** problem . . . .

"Wait!" cried Otto.

"We can't go **NOW!**"

"I can't find Tiger!!"

They searched EVERYWHERE.

Mom and Dad looked at the clock.
"We're going to miss the plane!"
they gasped.

They whisked Otto into the car.
And guess who
was there . . .

TIGER!

"Oh, thank goodness!"
said Mom. And off
they went.

DEPARTURES

At the airport, the line was **ENORMOUS.** But Otto was very, very patient.

Check-in 🧳
Please have your tickets ready.

Good boy!

At last, they fastened their seatbelts.
And—**zoooom!**

—up went the plane.

"Was it worth the wait, Otto?"
asked Dad.

But all Otto could say *now* was . . . .